New Moon

New Moon

by

Pegi Deitz Shea

Pictures by

Cathryn Falwell

BOYDS MILLS PRESS

Text copyright © 1996 by Pegi Deitz Shea
Illustrations copyright © 1996 by Cathryn Falwell

Published by Caroline House
Boyds Mills Press, Inc.
A Highlights Company
815 Church Street
Honesdale, Pennsylvania 18431
Printed in Mexico

Publisher Cataloging-in-Publication Data
Shea, Pegi Deitz.
New moon / by Pegi Deitz Shea ; illustrations by Cathryn Falwell.—1st ed.
[32]p. : col. ill. ; cm.
Summary : A young child looks for the moon on a dark winter night.
ISBN 1-56397-410-X
1. Moon—Fiction—Juvenile literature. 2. Winter—Fiction—Juvenile literature
[1. Moon—Fiction. 2. Winter—Fiction.] I. Falwell, Cathryn, ill. II. Title.
[E]—dc20   1996   AC   CIP
Library of Congress Catalog Card Number 95-83979

First edition, 1996
Book designed by Cathryn Falwell.
The text of this book is set in 18 point Garamond.
The illustrations are done in cut paper collage.

10 9 8 7 6 5 4 3 2 1

"Late yesterday,
I saw the new moon
with the old moon
in her arms."

*Adapted from
"The Ballad of Sir Patrick Spens"*

*To Mom and Dad,
who have jumped over
moons for me*

—P.D.S.

*For Neida,
and for Kyle & Katie*

—C.A.F.

One
clear night
in November,
I tugged Vincena's
high chair
over to the window.

I turned off
the light
and pointed up
to the sky.
"Look, Vinnie.
La luna.
Moooon."

As she lifted
her eyes,
the glow
of the full moon
fell over her.

And Vinnie —
who just learned
what the cow says —
whispered,
"Moooon."

The next night,
even before
she ate a
handful of rice,
Vinnie asked me,
"Moooon?"

"Well, let's see,"
I said,
and I pulled up
the blinds
and turned off
the light.

But all we saw
were trees swaying
and storm clouds
sweeping
across the sky.

"No moon tonight,"
I told Vinnie.
"No moon.
No moon," she said,
clanging her spoon
on the tray.

The next night
it poured.
I sang,
"The old man
is snoring."
But Vinnie
kept asking,
"Moon?"

"Moon went
bye-bye,"
I told her.
"No moon?
No moon?"
she cried.

So I read her
"Hey, Diddle Diddle."
I put a moon
on the floor and
we jumped over it,
back and forth.

Vinnie began
to find moons
in almost every
book she had.
"Moon!" She would
always show me.

Most of her moons
were like baseballs.
Sometimes
they looked
like Ds frontways
and backwards.

Once, I brought home
a schoolbook
to show her how
the moon changes.
Vinnie loved
all the moons.

But pictures
didn't glow the way
the real moon did
for Vinnie.
So we kept checking
every night.

"No moon.
No moon,"
Vinnie sighed,
leaving little
round moons
of wet air
on the window.

Then one day
I got off the bus
and ran
all the way home
to wake Vinnie up
from her nap.

There at the window,
we saw a shining slice
cutting its way
out of the clouds.

Vinnie had never
seen the moon
in the daytime.
"Moon?" she asked,
rubbing sleepies
from her eyes.

"Yes, yes!"
I said,
swinging her high.
"*La luna*
has come out
to play with you
while it's
still light."

"Moon!"
Vinnie crooned
as I tied down
her earflaps
and pulled up
her hood.

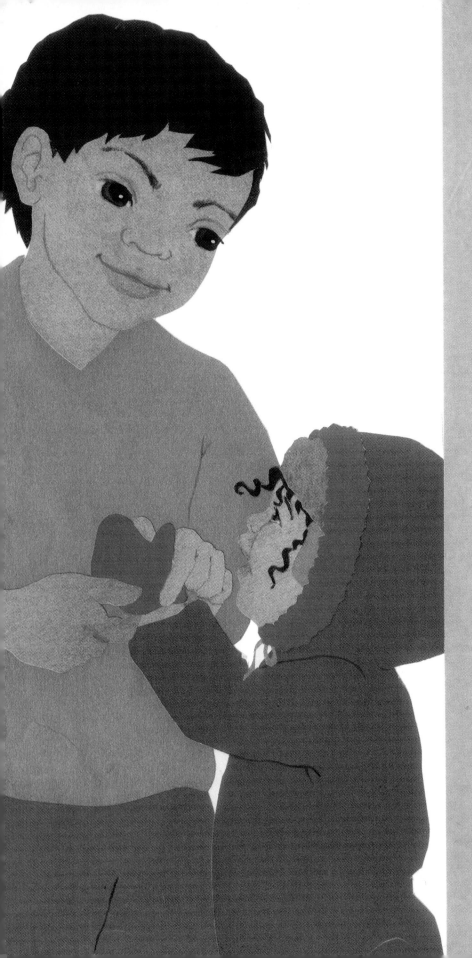

"Moon!"
she sang
as I stuck
her feet
into boots,
her hands
into mittens.

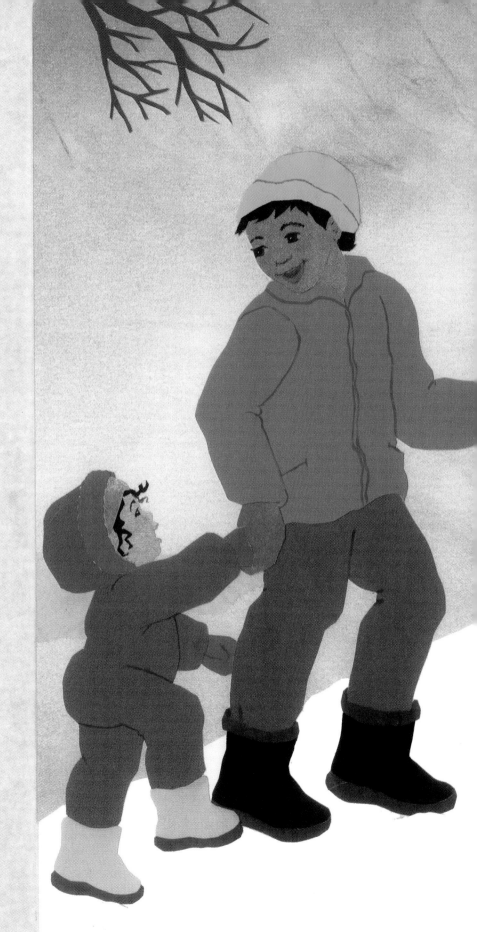

"Moon! Moon!"
she rang out
as we climbed
the hill
in the park
across the street.

When we got
to where
the trees stopped,
the daylight
was becoming
the color of
peach ice cream.

Vinnie leaned back
as far as she could
without tipping
in her snowsuit.
Her breath puffed
like a baby
whale's spout.

"Moooon,"
she whispered.
"Moooon,"
I whispered.

Vinnie hugged
one of my legs,
and we stood still
until the light
melted over
the faraway hills,

and
moon
was the
only
word
in
the
sky.